For Better or For Worse:®
Am I Too Big To Hug?

Lynn Johnston

TOR

A TOM DOHERTY ASSOCIATES BOOK
NEW YORK

This is a work of fiction. All the characters and events portrayed in this book are fictitious, and any resemblance to real people or events is purely coincidental.

FOR BETTER OR FOR WORSE®: AM I TOO BIG TO HUG?

FOR BETTER OR FOR WORSE® is a registered trademark of Lynn Johnston Productions, Inc. All rights reserved.

Copyright © 1992 by Lynn Johnston Productions, Inc. distributed internationally by Universal Press Syndicate.

A Tor Book
Published by Tom Doherty Associates, Inc.
175 Fifth Avenue
New York, N.Y. 10010

Tor® is a registered trademark of Tom Doherty Associates, Inc.

ISBN: 0-812-53640-1

First Tor edition: April 1994

Printed in the United States of America

0 9 8 7 6 5 4 3 2 1